DECONSTRUCTING POWERFUL SPEECHES

EMMA WATSON

UN GENDER EQUALITY SPEECH

REBECCA SJONGER

CRABTREE
PUBLISHING COMPANY
WWW.CRABTREEBOOKS.COM

CRABTREE
PUBLISHING COMPANY
WWW.CRABTREEBOOKS.COM

Author:
Rebecca Sjonger
Series research and development:
Janine Deschenes and Ellen Rodger
Editorial director:
Kathy Middleton
Editor:
Ellen Rodger
Proofreader:
Roseann Biederman
Graphic design:
Katherine Berti
Image research:
Rebecca Sjonger and Katherine Berti
Print coordinator:
Katherine Berti

Images:
Alamy
Chris Jobs: p. 19
Pacific Press Media Production Corp.: p. 17
UPI: P. 43 (top)
Associated Press, Matilde Campodonico: p. 5 (bottom)
digitalcollections.nypl.org, Screen Shot 2020-06-29 at 8.43.15 PM: p. 13 (inset bottom right)
Flickr
LSE Library: p. 29
Paul Kagame: p. 37 (top)
UN Photo, Mark Garten: p. 24 (top)
UN Women: p. 38 (bottom right)
UN Women, Simon Luethi: p. 7, 8–9
Getty Images, Taylor Hill: p. 41
Shutterstock
360b: p. 25 (center)
A Katz: p. 5 (top)
Anton Ivanov: p. 4 (top), 11 (top)
Cubankite: p. 38 (top right)
Dfree: p. 38 (bottom left)
Drop of Light: p. 6 (top)
Featureflash Photo Agency: p. 31
Kathy Hutchins: p. 12 (top left)
Lev Radin: p. 1
littlenySTOCK: p. 27
Martin Good: p. 34
monsoonclouds.net: p. 25 (top)
Nataly Reinch: p. 24 (bottom)
Osugi: p. 12 (bottom left), 28
quietbits: p. 30
Rena Schild: p. 6 (bottom)
Ryan Rodrick Beiler: p. 25 (bottom right)
Tinseltown: p. 3
twitter.com, Screen Shot 2020-06-30 at 9.35.14 AM: p. 18 (inset)
United Nations: p. 43 (left)
Wikimedia Commons
DFID, UK Department for International Development: p. 35
G 20: p. 36
Helene C. Stikkel: p. 34 (top)
Senator Chris Coons: p. 25 (bottom left)
US National Archives and Records Administration: p. 32
www.heforshe.org, Screen Shot 2020-07-10 at 1.49.51: p. 39 (inset)
www.loc.gov, Screen Shot 2020-06-29 at 3.30.56 PM: p. 10 (inset)
www.unwomen.org, Screen Shot 2020-07-10 at 3.44.56 PM: p. 40 (inset)
All other images by Shutterstock

Library and Archives Canada Cataloguing in Publication

Title: Emma Watson : UN gender equality speech / Rebecca Sjonger.
Names: Sjonger, Rebecca, author.
Series: Sjonger, Rebecca. Deconstructing powerful speeches.
Description: Series statement: Deconstructing powerful speeches | Includes bibliographical references and index.
Identifiers: Canadiana (print) 20200289527 | Canadiana (ebook) 20200289837 | ISBN 9780778781622 (softcover) | ISBN 9780778781585 (hardcover) | ISBN 9781427125880 (HTML)
Subjects: LCSH: Watson, Emma, 1990-—Oratory—Juvenile literature. | LCSH: Women's rights—Juvenile literature. | LCSH: Sex discrimination against women—Prevention—Juvenile literature. | LCSH: Speeches, addresses, etc., English—History and criticism—Juvenile literature. | LCSH: Oratory—Great Britain—Juvenile literature. | LCSH: Rhetoric—Juvenile literature.
Classification: LCC HQ1236 .S56 2021 | DDC j305.42—dc23

Library of Congress Cataloging-in-Publication Data

Names: Sjonger, Rebecca, author.
Title: Emma Watson : UN gender equality speech / Rebecca Sjonger.
Description: New York, NY : Crabtree Publishing Company, [2021] | Series: Deconstructing powerful speeches | Includes bibliographical references and index.
Identifiers: LCCN 2020031635 (print) | LCCN 2020031636 (ebook) | ISBN 9780778781585 (hardcover) | ISBN 9780778781622 (paperback) | ISBN 9781427125880 (ebook)
Subjects: LCSH: Watson, Emma, 1990---Juvenile literature. | Actresses--Political activity--Great Britain--Juvenile literature. | Feminism--Juvenile literature. | Speeches, addresses, etc. --Juvenile literature.
Classification: LCC PN2598.W25 S56 2021 (print) | LCC PN2598.W25 (ebook) | DDC 791.4302/8092--dc23
LC record available at https://lccn.loc.gov/2020031635
LC ebook record available at https://lccn.loc.gov/2020031636

Crabtree Publishing Company
www.crabtreebooks.com 1-800-387-7650

Printed in the U.S.A./092020/CG20200810

 In Canada: We acknowledge the financial support of the Government of Canada through the Canada Book Fund for our publishing activities.

Published in Canada
Crabtree Publishing
616 Welland Ave.
St. Catharines, Ontario
L2M 5V6

Published in the United States
Crabtree Publishing
347 Fifth Ave
Suite 1402-145
New York, NY 10016

Published in the United Kingdom
Crabtree Publishing
Maritime House
Basin Road North, Hove
BN41 1WR

Published in Australia
Crabtree Publishing
Unit 3 – 5 Currumbin Court
Capalaba
QLD 4157

CONTENTS

INTRODUCTION

Hundreds of fans waited outside the Legislative Palace in Montevideo, Uruguay. They hoped to spot British actor Emma Watson. Playing Hermione in the *Harry Potter* movies had made the 24-year-old famous. However, Watson was not in South America to promote her acting. She was there as a United Nations Women Goodwill Ambassador. She had represented UN Women in this way for two months. This was her first country visit on behalf of the international organization. When Watson saw the big crowd, she said it gave her "a feeling of excitement and gratitude." In her meetings with Uruguayan leaders that day in September 2014, she urged them to involve more women.

Emma Watson as Hermione

Legislative Palace, Montevideo, Uruguay

Phumzile Mlambo-Ngcuka was the Executive Director of UN Women. She explained that they asked for Watson's help because the young woman believed in equality. The actor also attracted a lot of attention from fans and the media. Watson influenced her **social media** following of over 14 million people. They crashed UN Women's website when her new role was announced. Even *Vogue* magazine reported on Watson's first official meeting in Montevideo. Mlambo-Ngcuka later said, "No one ever comes to see me."

A former deputy president of South Africa, Phumzile Mlambo-Ngcuka is the UN's Under-Secretary General and the Executive Director of UN Women.

Emma Watson is greeted with applause at the meeting in Uruguay.

UN headquarters, New York City, U.S.

HEFORSHE CAMPAIGN

Just a few days later, Emma Watson drew more attention at the launch of HeForShe. UN Women planned the event to "kick-start a global **solidarity** movement in support of women's rights and full equality between women and men." It was held on the evening of Saturday, September 20, 2014. An impressive audience gathered at the UN headquarters in New York City. They included **ambassadors** from UN member nations, leaders from UN organizations, politicians, and other **notable** guests.

Wolf Blitzer is a journalist with CNN.

BIG-NAME SPEAKERS

Emma Watson and Wolf Blitzer co-hosted the event. Blitzer welcomed everyone and introduced the speakers. They were shown live on a global webcast. UN Secretary-General Ban Ki-moon delivered the first speech. He described the crisis of **human rights** abuses and the need for change. Ban joked about Watson's part in the *Harry Potter* series: "She's been wielding a magic wand in a movie. I hope you will use your magic wand to stop violence against women!" Phumzile Mlambo-Ngcuka spoke next. She described examples of inequality between women and men around the world.

Emma Watson used her popularity and influence to help launch the UN's HeForShe campaign.

WATSON'S TURN

When Wolf Blitzer introduced Emma Watson, she rose from her seat between the UN Secretary-General and the President of the **General Assembly**. The audience applauded as she approached the front of the hall. Upbeat music played in the background. A red HeForShe banner hung from the front of the podium where Watson took her place to speak. A large logo hung on top of heavy black curtains behind her. It was also pinned to the lapel of Watson's silver-gray coat dress.

GENDER INEQUALITY

Emma Watson's speech highlighted **gender inequality**. Gender relates to the social expectations taken on by people born female or male. They are often taught to have distinct characteristics and roles. Most cultures expect boys and girls to behave differently. Traditional beliefs about gender affect the rights of girls and women worldwide. Human rights are basic freedoms due to all people.

At the launch, Phumzile Mlambo-Ngcuka said, "When women are empowered, the whole of humanity benefits."

President of United Nations General Assembly, Sam Kahamba Kutesa

UN Women Goodwill Ambassador Emma Watson

Men have held more power and had more prospects than women throughout history. Today, over two-thirds of business leaders and three-quarters of national government leaders are men. In many places, boys get better access to health care and more nutritious foods. Girls are less likely to go to school or take training programs. This makes it harder for them to get a good job. They are paid less for doing the same work. Unfair treatment based on things like race, age, or gender is **discrimination**.

AN INVITATION

Fighting discrimination and gender inequality is one of the missions of the UN. It aims to end gender inequality by 2030. Emma Watson used her speech to invite boys and men to join this new international gender equality movement. She announced the UN's goal to engage one billion of them. The need to act was urgent. It still is today, which is why Watson's speech continues to inspire people.

Madam Yoo (Ban) Soon-taek

Actor Kiefer Sutherland

Ban Ki-moon thanked the audience for its commitment to protecting human rights. He said, "What a power and energy I am feeling!"

READ IT

Emma Watson's **address** to the UN was over 1,200 words long. Sources like this book and most websites focus on key sections of it. To read the full text, visit **https://bit.ly/3i9MCXo**

WATCH IT

See Emma Watson deliver the speech: **www.youtube.com/watch?v=gkjW9PZBRfk**

PERSUASIVE PRIMARY SOURCES

Emma Watson's speech is an original, firsthand account. This is called a primary source. These materials include a wide variety of text, audio, and images. Photos of Watson and the movies she acts in are primary sources. Other examples include opinion polls, marriage certificates, and other records that list data. Primary sources bring us as close as we can get to being at a historical event or in a time period. Watson's speech at the United Nations gives us a look at the fight for gender equality in the early 2000s.

SECONDARY SOURCES

Secondary sources interpret, or explain, original materials. They rely on the information found in one or more primary sources. Secondary sources might **analyze** an event, consider someone else's ideas, or express an opinion. For example, reviews of the *Harry Potter* movies are secondary sources. Textbooks used in schools and newspaper articles are other common examples. These sources can be made some time after the original source was created. This means they can provide more background and sum up ideas.

The U.S. ***Library of Congress*** *is the second largest library in the world. It calls primary sources "raw materials."*

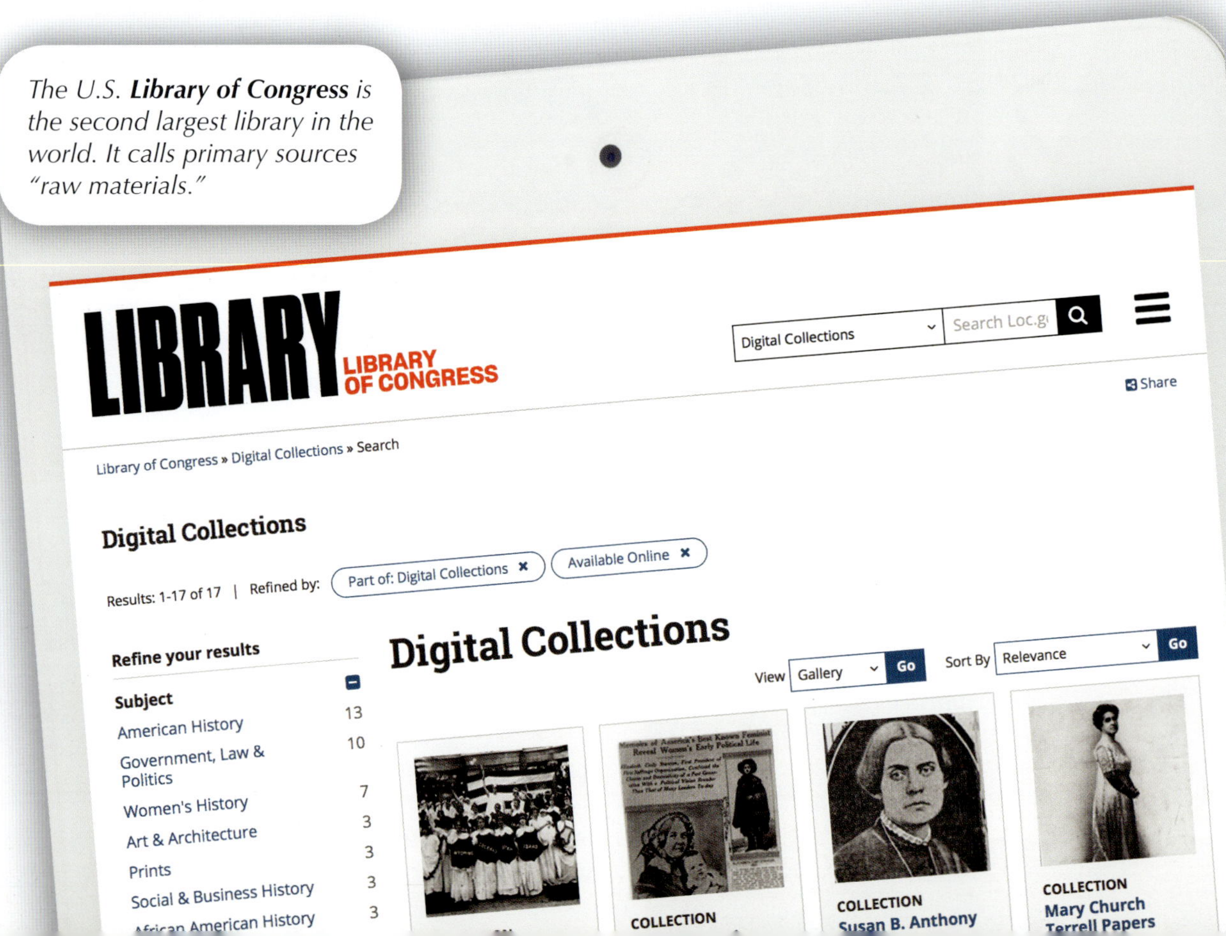

primary sources

Have you ever made a video? If so, you created a primary source!

SOURCE ANALYSIS 101

Get the basic details from a primary source first, then analyze them. Gather as much information as possible. Start with:

Maker, such as a writer

***Intended** audience*

Date it was created

*Purpose or **argument***

Place it was delivered

Maker's point of view

Your excellencies, UN Secretary-General, President of the General Assembly, Executive Director of UN Women, and distinguished guests...

Today, we are launching a campaign called HeForShe. I am reaching out to you because we need your help. We want to end gender inequality—and to do this we need everyone involved...

Statesman Edmund Burke said: "All that is needed for the forces of evil to triumph is for enough good men and women to do nothing."

Watson paused to look at each person she named; live webcast meant there was also a worldwide audience

Purpose was to get support for HeForShe and its goal of equality for all

Watson shared this eighteenth-century quotation to explain her own views

Speaker: *Emma Watson*
Audience: *Millions worldwide*
Date: *September 20, 2014*

COLLECTING DETAILS

Emma Watson's speech is recent and well documented online. However, it is not always so easy to find information about a primary source. If specific details are known, they may be found in databases. These are collections of facts and figures kept by libraries and other organizations. They gather information about each source in their holdings.

New York Public Library digital collections

DIGGING DEEPER

Many people spoke at the HeForShe launch. However, Emma Watson's speech got the most attention. What are the benefits of having a celebrity speaker?

PUSHING FOR CHANGE

One reason people give speeches is to push for change. They often present a specific point of view about one issue. Emma Watson used her speech to boost awareness of gender equality. Her words were chosen to convince the audience to think a certain way. Like many **persuasive** speakers, Watson used the following features.

Speechwriters try to choose just the right words to make an argument.

MAKING AN ARGUMENT

CLAIM

Speeches support their arguments with claims, which are statements or conclusions.

Women are paid less than men for doing the same work.

EVIDENCE

Evidence is data or facts that prove the claims are true.

Men with full-time jobs make about 25 percent more than women who work full time.

WARRANT

Warrants connect evidence and claims to support a course of action.

If women and men do the exact same work, then they should be paid the same amount.

APPEAL

Appeals in speeches urge the audience to act.

Employers must start paying men and women equally today!

INFLUENCING THE AUDIENCE

Rhetoric is the art of **persuasion** used in speeches and many other texts. Rhetorical language convinces the audience using three main strategies.

LOGOS

Logos asks the audience to consider logic, or reason. In a speech, logos may begin with a general idea that is supported by facts. It could also use these facts as a starting point and draw conclusions.

All workers deserve to be treated equally. It does not make sense to pay two people different amounts if they do the same job.

ETHOS

Ethos urges the audience to believe the speaker because of his or her good character. This may be done by sharing personal experiences, finding common ground, or showing respect.

You and I both work hard to earn a living. I am sure you would agree that everyone should be paid fairly for their efforts.

PATHOS

Pathos plays on the audience's emotions to win them over.

When women are paid less than men, it reveals that they are still ***second-class*** *citizens who do not receive fair and equal treatment.*

Anyone can use rhetorical language to strengthen the claims, evidence, and warrants in their speeches.

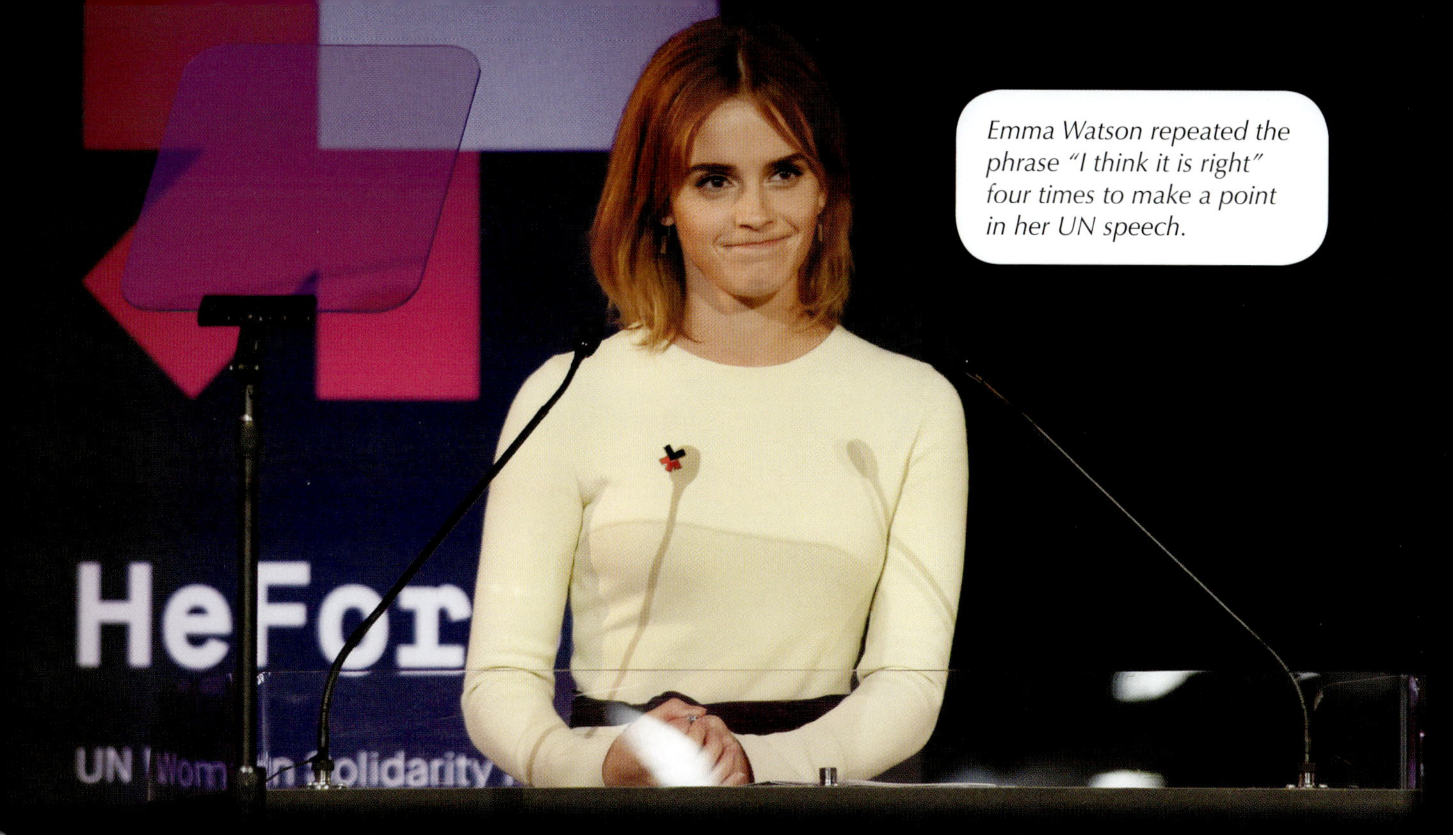

Emma Watson repeated the phrase "I think it is right" four times to make a point in her UN speech.

WORDS THAT WORK

Speakers use rhetorical language in different ways. They may also use rhetorical devices, such as:

- Figurative language, such as **metaphors** and **similes**
- Comparing two unalike things in an **analogy**
- Repeating key words and phrases
- Exaggerating in **hyperboles**
- Giving things human qualities through **personification**
- Making some facts sound less important than they really are

DIGGING DEEPER

Before audio and video recordings existed, it was difficult to prove what a speaker really said. What problems could this pose for studying a speech?

HEARD NOT READ

The spoken word makes speeches powerful. Reading the words silently is a different experience. Emma Watson used language and voice together to deliver her argument. Depending on how the speaker uses his or her voice, the same words can take on different meanings. Diction is the way someone pronounces and produces the sounds in words. It also includes the words a speaker or writer chooses to use. The tone in which words are said can also change their effect. The rising and falling rhythms of those tones are called cadence. Along with emphasis, all these things helped Watson make her points. She spoke carefully and thoughtfully. Despite being a famous actor, she admitted to being nervous. Her voice revealed her feelings at times during the speech.

CHAPTER 2

WORDS AND MEANING

Deconstructing a speech means looking at it **critically**. This helps uncover a speaker's goals. The first step is to review the whole primary source. Note how the information is presented. Look for the parts of an argument and rhetorical language. Studying these elements in Emma Watson's speech shows how she felt about gender equality. She was clearly in favor of it and passionate about the HeForShe movement.

PRESENTING IDEAS

Like many speakers, Emma Watson used comparison and contrast to help make her case. In contrast to many girls around the world, her parents and teachers did not see her as being less worthy than a boy. She called herself "one of the lucky ones." Watson also compared the ways mothers and fathers are viewed. "I've seen my father's role as a parent being valued less by society, despite my needing his presence as a child as much as my mother's," she said. Sequencing places facts and ideas in order, especially when listing events. Watson used this style when she shared her experiences as a young girl, a teen, and an adult. The causal way of arranging information looks at causes and effects. For example, Watson noted, "If men don't have to control, women won't have to be controlled."

SPEAKER SPOTLIGHT

Emma Watson's large number of fans was one reason UN Women wanted her to be a goodwill ambassador. She was also active on social media. This allowed her to promote HeForShe and other projects widely. On January 23, 2015, a young woman tagged Watson on a Twitter post. It read: "my dad says I can't be a engineer 'cause it's a 'men profession' what do I do to change that?" Watson replied, "Become an engineer." Her brilliant answer was retweeted thousands of times. It also received worldwide media attention.

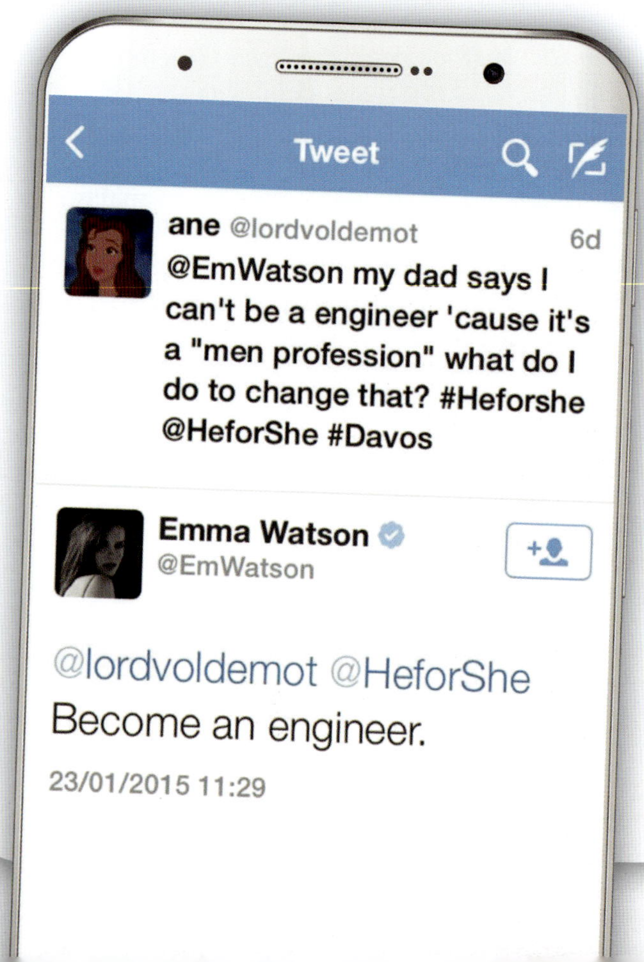

The media reported differently on what Emma Watson wore and said than it did with her male co-stars.

PURPOSE

The purpose of a speech is the reason for making it. Emma Watson appeared at the UN event to help launch its HeForShe movement. Her speech encouraged men and boys everywhere to support change and promote equality for all. Watson went beyond the inequality that girls and women faced, however. Her argument stated ways that boys and men were also trapped in traditional gender roles.

DECONSTRUCT IT

To determine the purpose of a speech, listen to it or read it and ask:

- What is the speaker's central argument?
- Who is the speaker trying to appeal to?

Speaker: *Emma Watson*
Audience: *Millions worldwide*
Date: *September 20, 2014*

*I want men to take up this **mantle**, so that their daughters, sisters, and mothers can be free from **prejudice**, but also so that their sons have permission to be **vulnerable and human** too…and in doing so be a more true and complete version of themselves… I am inviting you to step forward, to be seen, and to ask yourself: **if not me, who? If not now, when?***

Responsibility

Being treated unfairly

Rejected these being for just one gender

Quoted Hillel, an ancient Jewish religious leader

DIGGING DEEPER

Can you think of any examples of prejudice, or unfair treatment, from your own life?

Traditionally, society expects different genders to take on different roles.

CLAIMS AND EVIDENCE

Emma Watson backed her arguments with claims and evidence. These were influenced by her well-informed audience, the modern time period, and the UN setting. Watson made bold conclusions and shared data to prove action was needed. For example, she stated that many men did not seek treatment for mental illness. As measurable proof, Watson noted that men aged 20 to 49 in the United Kingdom were more likely to kill themselves than to die any other way. She claimed it was not considered manly to get help. This was a direct result of gender inequality.

DECONSTRUCT IT

To find claims and evidence in a speech, ask:

- What conclusions are being made?
- Which facts or data support these statements?
- Does the speaker use voice, such as emphasis or pacing, to reinforce any text?

Speaker: *Emma Watson*
Audience: *Millions worldwide*
Date: *September 20, 2014*

> *...the reality is that if we do nothing, it will take 75 years, or **for me to be nearly a hundred before women can expect to be paid the same as men**—for the same work. **15.5 million girls will be married** in the next 16 years **as children**. And at current rates it won't be until 2086 before all rural African girls can have a secondary education.*

Paused to allow this fact to sink in

Being forced into early marriage is a huge gender inequality issue

Used voice for emphasis

BEHIND THE WORDS

Emma Watson referred to a variety of human rights in her speech. **Equal pay** is an issue in North America and around the world. Another problem is girls and young women being forced to marry. This is more common in Africa and South Asia. Some cultures and families struggling with **poverty** see girls as a burden to pass off. For the same reasons, many girls are not sent to high school or university. This inequality limits their futures. At the time, things were improving—but not fast enough according to Watson.

DIGGING DEEPER

Do you think girls and boys are treated equally in your own family, school, or community? Why or why not?

WARRANTS AND APPEALS

Emma Watson connected her claims and evidence in warrants. These statements upheld an appeal. Watson used them to urge the audience to support HeForShe. This request for action was her main appeal.

DECONSTRUCT IT

Find warrants and appeals in a speech by asking:

- Is the speaker urging the audience to act or think a certain way?
- How are claims and evidence being connected to convince them?

Speaker: *Emma Watson*
Audience: *Millions worldwide*
Date: *September 20, 2014*

*Men: **I would like to take this opportunity to extend your formal invitation**. Gender equality is your issue too…We don't often talk about men being **imprisoned** by **gender stereotypes**, but I can see that that they are and that **when they are free, things will change for women as a natural consequence**.*

Said with humor since they should not have to be asked

Trapped

Traditional roles

Example of cause and effect

IMPACT 10x10x10 focused on leaders who had the most power to make change worldwide.

WATCH IT

Check out the video of Emma Watson speaking at the World Economic Forum at: **www.youtube.com/watch?v=oE28bb11GQs**

SPEAKER SPOTLIGHT

Emma Watson introduced a HeForShe program called IMPACT 10x10x10 on January 23, 2015. The launch took place at the World Economic Forum in Davos, Switzerland. This annual meeting brings together international business and political leaders. The next phase of the movement focused on engaging these people. Ban Ki-moon and Phumzile Mlambo-Ngcuka as well as others connected to the UN joined Watson on stage. She noted that some people wondered what they should do after committing to the movement. Watson explained, "The truth is the 'What now?' is down to you. What your HeForShe commitment will be is personal and there is no best way. Everything is valid." She also encouraged supporters to share their experiences on social media.

The future for girls depends partly on equality in education and opportunities. Today, women make up half of the world's population and hold only 23 percent of the seats in parliaments and senates throughout the world.

Ellen Johnson Sirleaf, President of Liberia (2006-2018)

Angela Merkel, Chancellor of Germany

Nancy Pelosi, Speaker of the United States House of Representatives

RHETORICAL LANGUAGE

Speeches use rhetorical language to make claims, support them with evidence, and make appeals and warrants. Emma Watson used logos to ask the audience to consider logic and reason. Pathos drew them in and helped to persuade them that inequality was wrong. Ethos allowed Watson to find common ground with them and boost her **credibility**.

DECONSTRUCT IT

To identify the rhetorical language in a speech, ask:

- How is the speaker using logic and reason to persuade the audience?
- Does the speaker's character help support the central argument?
- How is the audience being swayed by emotion?

logos

Speaker: *Emma Watson*
Audience: *Millions worldwide*
Date: *September 20, 2014*

*I think it is right that I am paid the same as my male counterparts. **I think it is right that** I should be able to **make decisions about my own body**. I think it is right that **women be involved on my behalf** in the **policies** and decisions that will affect my life. I think it is right that socially I am afforded the same respect as men.*

Used repetition to reinforce the logic of her conclusions

Referred to reproductive rights

Government leaders

Rules and plans

pathos

Speaker: *Emma Watson*
Audience: *Millions worldwide*
Date: *September 20, 2014*

*When I was eight, I was confused at being called "bossy," because I wanted to direct the plays we would put on for our parents—**but the boys were not**...When at 15, my girlfriends started dropping out of their beloved sports teams because **they didn't want to appear "muscly."** When at 18, my male friends **were unable to express their feelings**.*

Shook her head to highlight the inequality

Emphasized gender norms **as persuasive strategy**

Played to the audience's own emotions

ethos

You might be thinking who is this ***Harry Potter girl****, and what is she doing speaking at the UN,* ***and it's a really good question****….in my moments of doubt, I've told myself firmly—****if not me, who, if not now, when****. If you have similar doubts when opportunities are presented to you, I hope that those words will be helpful.*

Speaker: *Emma Watson*
Audience: *Millions worldwide*
Date: *September 20, 2014*

Watson played Hermione in the movies

Audience laughed, which showed she had found common ground

Repeated this Hillel quote

SPEAKER SPOTLIGHT

On September 20, 2016, HeForShe celebrated its second anniversary. The event was held at the Museum of Modern Art in New York City. Emma Watson spoke briefly to the audience of supporters. She presented evidence to prove the movement's successes so far. For example, over one million people had pledged support. She listed some of the notable people who had made commitments. This included "the entire EU commission, the NATO Secretary-General, the President of the International Olympic Committee, numerous heads of state and politicians from around the world… everyone from Usain Bolt to Tom Hanks..." Watson chose these details to give her argument credibility and trustworthiness.

WATCH IT

See Emma Watson's HeForShe anniversary speech:
www.youtube.com/watch?v=N6AK6tN2P-o&t=213s

ANALYZING PERSPECTIVES

A speech often reveals how the maker felt about an issue. Emma Watson shared her perspective, or point of view, in her UN address. She believed that women and men were equal, so they should be treated that way. Wolf Blitzer, her co-host, agreed. He kicked off the HeForShe launch by declaring, "I say what all of you say: it is about time." Based on the audience's responses during the event, they agreed. They interrupted Watson's speech to applaud multiple times. Their perspectives reflected a section of society's views at the time, too. A speaker may also show how he or she feels about the audience. The way Watson presented herself and addressed the group in the UN General Assembly Hall showed her respect for them.

UN headquarters, New York City, USA

DECONSTRUCT IT

To determine a speaker's point of view, ask:

- How could the speaker's perspective be summed up in one sentence?
- How does the language used show the speaker's feelings?

Speaker: *Emma Watson*
Audience: *Millions worldwide*
Date: *September 20, 2014*

> *Both men and women should feel free to be* ***sensitive****. Both men and women should feel free to be* ***strong****. It is time that we all* ***perceive*** *gender on a* ***spectrum*** *instead of two sets of* ***opposing ideals****.*

- **Chose words usually linked to one gender**
- **See previous**
- **Identify or understand**
- **A wide range**
- **Audience burst into applause**

A POINT IN HISTORY

Both the maker and the audience are products of their time. One hundred years before Emma Watson's speech, women in most places around the world were treated like second-class citizens. They could not vote or own property. Supporters of women's rights fought hard for social, political, and economic equality. They were called feminists. Progress was made in many countries over the decades. There was still much to be done globally, though. The HeForShe movement was meant to help carry on these historical efforts.

Suffragettes were women who fought for the right to vote. Suffrage means the right to vote in elections.

CHOOSING WORDS

Sometimes, a writer creates a speech on behalf of the person who delivers it. The writer aims to present the speaker's perspective. Public figures like Emma Watson often use professional writers to help them sound their best. However, Watson wrote her own speech. In later interviews, she described the pressure she faced not to use the word "feminism" as she drafted it. In her speech, she noted that it was now connected with "man-hating". People avoided using the term for this reason. This did not make sense to Watson. She saw feminism as "the belief that men and women should have equal rights and opportunities".

> *"...feminism has become an unpopular word. Women are choosing not to identify as feminists. Apparently, I am among the ranks of women whose expressions are seen as* ***too strong, too aggressive, isolating, and anti-men, unattractive even****."*

Speaker: *Emma Watson*
Audience: *Millions worldwide*
Date: *September 20, 2014*

Listed common complaints people made against feminists

The Fearless Girl statue was originally located near the Charging Bull statue near the New York Stock Exchange building in New York City, but later moved. It was commissioned by a company that sold stock in companies with a high number of women in senior leadership roles.

SPEAKER SPOTLIGHT

British radio and TV host Greg James interviewed Emma Watson on March 8, 2015. It was broadcast live from Facebook's office in London, England. Viewers around the world were watching online. Watson took part on behalf of UN Women in honor of International Women's Day. She appeared to have considered James's questions in advance. Watson sometimes referred to papers before responding to him. These replies may have been written by her or by someone else. Watson's answers reflected her own perspective, however. She took a firm stance on feminism and people's reluctance to identify with the movement. "If you stand for equality, then you're a feminist. Sorry to tell you, you're a feminist," she said.

Greg James referred to Emma Watson's "sensational" HeForShe speech in his interview.

WATCH IT

Greg James and Emma Watson's conversation can be viewed on Facebook: **www.facebook.com/watch/?v=1032777126741177**

DIGGING DEEPER

Do you think a speechwriter and a speaker need to share the same point of view? Why or why not?

REVEALING TRANSCRIPTS

A transcript is a printed version of a primary source. Sometimes, it is the only form available to study. If possible, compare the spoken words in a recording to the official transcript. This may reveal some interesting details. In the printed version of Emma Watson's speech, she says, "I don't know if I am qualified to be here." She never said this aloud at the UN event, though. This raises questions: Was it in her original written speech notes? If so, why did she choose not to say it? If not, who added it and why? The transcript also reveals an error made in Watson's speech. It states that Hillary Clinton spoke in Beijing in 1995, but Watson said it was 1997. The earlier year is correct. Watson may have simply misspoken, or she got the year wrong and someone fixed it later.

DIGGING DEEPER

How could studying all the available versions of a speech help with analyzing it?

First Lady Hillary Clinton delivered a speech called "Women's Rights Are Human Rights" in China in 1995.

LIMITED PERSPECTIVE

Primary sources often present only one perspective about an issue. A speaker may leave out facts that do not help his or her argument. This limits what we can learn from them. Many factors shape someone's point of view. Emma Watson was born and raised in Europe. She started her acting career as a child and had been famous for more than half of her life. Earlier in 2014, she had graduated from Brown University. This is a prestigious American school. All these experiences, plus the fact that she was a white woman, helped form her perspective. Some people disagreed with her representing UN Women and HeForShe because of her **privileged** background. Others pointed out that Watson's speech did not mention **transgender** people. They felt she should have been more inclusive.

Speaker: *Emma Watson*
Audience: *Millions worldwide*
Date: *September 20, 2014*

> "*No country in the world can yet say that they have achieved gender equality...**If we stop defining each other by what we are not and start defining ourselves by who we are,** we can all be freer and this is what HeForShe is about. It's about **freedom**.*"

DIGGING DEEPER

How might people's personal experiences influence their perspectives?

DECONSTRUCT IT

To find the limitations of a speech, ask:

- How does the maker's perspective shape this primary source?
- Are any important facts being left out?
- Based on evidence from other sources, are there any points that should be explored further?

Some secondary sources called out HeForShe for ignoring non-traditional gender issues

UN members held very different perspectives about personal freedoms

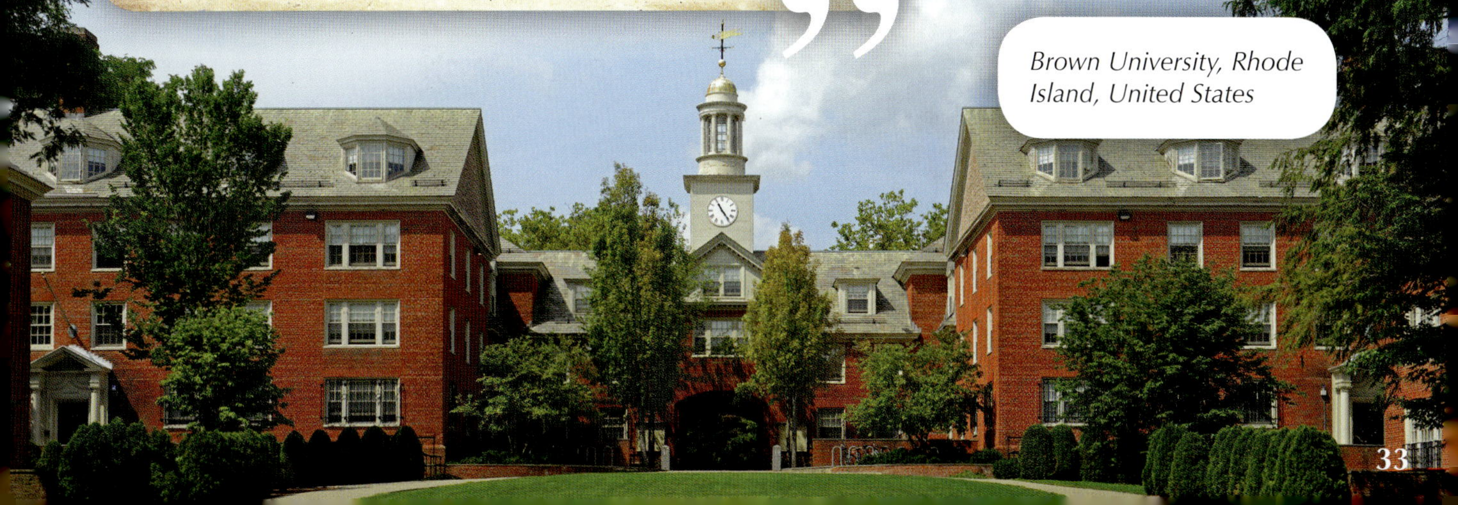

Brown University, Rhode Island, United States

BEHIND THE WORDS

Emma Watson did not refer to any disagreement about equality in her speech. Almost 200 countries are members of the United Nations. Each has its own view on women's rights and equality. There were leaders in the hall whose countries would not support the freedoms promoted by HeForShe.

OTHER PERSPECTIVES

The makers of speeches are not the only ones with a point of view. The people who create secondary sources have their own **biases** and perspectives. This can lead to multiple ways of looking at the same speech or issue. It is important to study other primary and secondary sources to get a better understanding of gender equality. These materials could be from the same time period or in response to the speech. Studying them helps create a broader picture.

President Isaias Afwerki has ruled Eritrea since 1993. Like many countries, it is a member of the UN despite its poor human rights record.

United Nations Office at Geneva, Switzerland

NOT ONE SIZE FITS ALL

Malala Yousafzai of Pakistan fought for the right for girls to be educated. That is why the Taliban shot her on a school bus when she was 15 years old. The Islamic **fundamentalist** group wanted to silence her. However, she survived to tell her story. She wrote a book called *I Am Malala*. Yousafzai started the Malala Fund. It helps girls in developing countries get an education. She was passionate about girls' rights—but she did not view herself as a feminist. Emma Watson's speech changed her mind. Yousafzai talked about it at the World Economic Forum in Davos, Switzerland. She was interviewed in front of an audience of world leaders on January 25, 2018. Like Watson, Yousafzai argued for gender equality. But her perspective on how to achieve this goal differed. Instead of HeForShe, Yousafzai believed that girls and women would "do it ourselves."

Emma Watson and Malala Yousafzai have met and discussed feminism and equality. In 2014, Malala Yousafzai was the youngest person ever to receive the Nobel Peace Prize.

I was seeing that feminism was ***controversial*** *and that feminism was* ***women's superiority****... I realized that feminism is just another word for equality...I said it long ago at the UN that first we wanted men to do something for us, but that time is gone now.* ***We're not going to ask men to change the world****...We are going to stand up for ourselves, we are going to raise our voices, and we are going to change the world.*

Something that divided opinions

Some view it as women gaining power over men

Different from HeForShe's perspective

Speaker: *Malala Yousafzai*
Audience: *World Economic Forum*
Date: *January 25, 2018*

WATCH IT

See Malala Yousafzai speak at the World Economic Forum: **https://bit.ly/2YBj6SD**

BUSINESS PERSPECTIVE

Canadian Prime Minister Justin Trudeau delivered a speech at the same World Economic Forum as Malala Yousafzai. He addressed global leaders in Davos on January 23, 2018. Trudeau spoke in Canada's two official languages: English and French. He urged the audience full of powerful people to do their part to improve gender equality. The Canadian prime minister appealed to them with a business-based argument. He focused on the benefits for world economies when women are empowered. Trudeau relied on **statistics** to share his point of view. For example, he claimed that "narrowing the gender gap in Canada could add $150 billion to our economy by 2026". His perspective was that governments had to change the ways they did things in order to reach the goal of gender equality.

Canadian Prime Minister Justin Trudeau made Malala Yousafzai an honorary Canadian in 2017 for her girls' rights work.

Speaker: *Justin Trudeau*
Audience: *World Economic Forum*
Date: *January 23, 2018*

> *I'm talking about* ***hiring, promoting, and retaining more women****. And not just because it's the right thing to do, or the nice thing to do, but because* ***it's the smart thing to do****...More women in leadership positions won't just grow our* ***economy****, create jobs, and strengthen our communities. It will also lead to* ***innovation and change*** *in the workplace...*

The key was to give women in the workplace more power

This perspective focused on how equality benefited everyone

Resources and wealth of each country

Diverse points of view lead to new ways of doing things

WATCH IT

Justin Trudeau's 2018 speech in Davos is online at: **www.youtube.com/watch?v=207JmWKBNNM**

World Economic Forum, January 23, 2018

Emma Watson awarded scholarships in her name to young activists at the One Young World Summit in Ottawa, Canada.

CHAPTER 4

INFLUENCES THEN AND NOW

The audience at the United Nations rose to give Emma Watson a standing ovation when she finished speaking. The Secretary-General and the President of the Assembly both shook her hand before she sat down. Wolf Blitzer returned to the stage. He exclaimed, "What a beautiful, beautiful speech…" A variety of other speakers and presentations followed. For example, actor Kiefer Sutherland introduced a video of "extraordinary everyday men" who supported the new movement. It showed them holding up #HeForShe signs. Later, actor Meghan Markle introduced 13-year-old cellist Sujari Britt. The teen played for the audience. As the evening wrapped up, Watson and Phumzile Mlambo-Ngcuka returned to the podium. The goodwill ambassador and the Executive Director of UN Women thanked everyone for joining them and supporting HeForShe. Watson concluded, "It's been one of the best days of my life."

Kiefer Sutherland

Meghan Markle

Sujari Britt

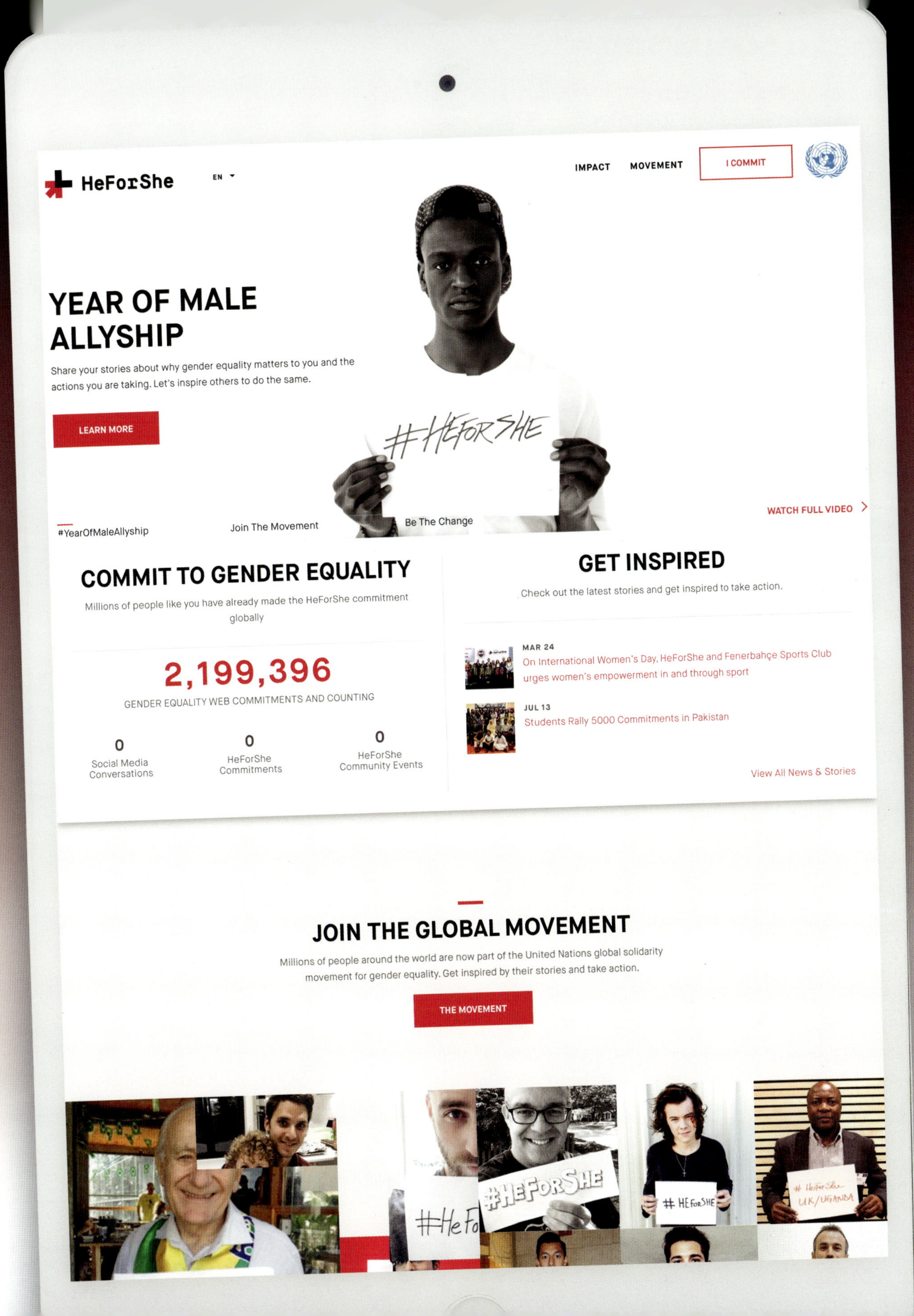
HeForShe
EN
IMPACT
MOVEMENT
I COMMIT
YEAR OF MALE ALLYSHIP
Share your stories about why gender equality matters to you and the actions you are taking. Let's inspire others to do the same.
LEARN MORE
#HEFORSHE
#YearOfMaleAllyship
Join The Movement
Be The Change
WATCH FULL VIDEO
COMMIT TO GENDER EQUALITY
Millions of people like you have already made the HeForShe commitment globally
2,199,396
GENDER EQUALITY WEB COMMITMENTS AND COUNTING
0
Social Media Conversations
0
HeForShe Commitments
0
HeForShe Community Events
GET INSPIRED
Check out the latest stories and get inspired to take action.
MAR 24
On International Women's Day, HeForShe and Fenerbahçe Sports Club urges women's empowerment in and through sport
JUL 13
Students Rally 5000 Commitments in Pakistan
View All News & Stories
JOIN THE GLOBAL MOVEMENT
Millions of people around the world are now part of the United Nations global solidarity movement for gender equality. Get inspired by their stories and take action.
THE MOVEMENT
#HEFORSHE
HEForSHE
HeForShe UK/UGANDA

GLOBAL COMMITMENTS

At the launch, Secretary-General Ki-moon was the first person to pledge his commitment to the movement. He signed up using the HeForShe website. The rest of the men in the UN hall were also urged to go to the website and show their support right away. Following the event, the international media gave Emma Watson's speech a great deal of attention. It was mainly very positive. This coverage helped raise global awareness of HeForShe. An online map showed the locations of boys and men around the world who committed to supporting gender equality. Today, the website shows that just over two million commitments have been made. This is far short of the goal. The site shows a much higher number—over one billion—for social media mentions about the movement.

MOVING FORWARD

Emma Watson continued to support HeForShe as a spokesperson for the movement. On September 30, 2016, she appeared at the One Young World Summit in Ottawa, Canada. Watson told the audience about giving her speech at the UN—and what happened next. "I was very nervous before that speech. The nerves were followed by a tremendous high immediately afterwards and a crushing low a few days after that. My best hopes and my worst fears were confirmed all at once. I had opened Pandora's box to a standing ovation and almost simultaneously a level of critique I had never experienced in my life...It was my scary first step as an activist, a word I never imagined I would use to describe myself," she said. Watson encouraged the audience of young people to work together to change the world.

DIGGING DEEPER

The number of commitments to HeForShe has not been as high as expected. Does this mean Emma Watson's speech was not successful? Why or why not?

Emma Watson continues to support feminist causes. In 2020, she teamed with British author Reni Eddo-Lodge and the Women of the World Foundation on a project. The project honors the history of women, transgender people, and those who don't identify as one gender in the city of London, U.K.

MODERN PERSPECTIVE

At the beginning of 2017, António Guterres became the new UN Secretary-General. He was one of nine speakers at an International Women's Day event held on March 8, 2019. A variety of musicians also performed. The audience, including members of the media, gathered in the Economic and Social Council Chamber at the UN Headquarters in New York City. Guterres told them that he viewed gender equality as "a question of power." His perspective was that men had "ignored, silenced and oppressed women for centuries—even millennia." He warned that change would be difficult to achieve.

WATCH IT

Read the full text of António Guterres's speech: **https://bit.ly/3eEhcGj**

Speaker: *António Guterres*
Audience: *Attendants of the International Women's Day event held at the UN Headquarters in New York City*
Date: *March 8, 2019*

"*In recent decades, we have seen remarkable progress on women's rights and leadership. But these gains are* ***far from consistent****. And they have sparked a backlash from an* ***entrenched patriarchy****...Women's political representation in parliaments around the world stands at less than 25 percent.* ***At the highest levels that drops to 9 percent****...just one-quarter of the subjects of news stories are women, and most often as victims rather than leaders. Despite women's achievements and successes,* ***their voices are still routinely overlooked, and their opinions ignored****... At present trends, it will take* ***two centuries*** *to close the gap in* ***economic empowerment****—a gap that is widening, not lessening, by the day. I do not accept a world that tells my granddaughters that economic equality can wait for their granddaughter's granddaughters. I know you agree: Our world cannot wait...*"

Room for improvement exists in every country

Deep-rooted system of men being in charge

In other words, 91 out of 100 presidents, prime ministers, and other top leaders are men

In the workplace and in society

The year 2219

Financial equality

DID IT HELP?

Some people called Emma Watson's speech a game-changer. It did get a lot of attention. In the end, however, it did not change much for women's rights. The most recent reports from UN Women suggest that gender inequality is actually getting worse. In 2016, the UN launched the 2030 Agenda for Sustainable Development. This action plan includes 17 Sustainable Development Goals (SDGs). Goal 5 calls for the world to "Achieve gender equality and empower all women and girls." It lists targets for things such as health care, education, and employment. Change will only come when the whole world pulls together to meet measurable goals like these ones.

BIBLIOGRAPHY

INTRODUCTION

"Emma Watson calls for more women in politics in Uruguay." *The Sun Daily*, September 18, 2014. https://bit.ly/2ZhmBwy

"Emma Watson: Gender equality is your issue too." UN Women. https://bit.ly/3dE1QR5

"Emma Watson HeForShe Speech at the United Nations." YouTube. www.youtube.com/watch?v=Q0Dg226G2Z8&feature=youtu.be

"Emma Watson 'touched' by reception in Uruguay." *Washington Examiner*, September 17, 2014. https://washex.am/3i3BICt

"Executive Director Phumzile Mlambo-Ngcuka." UN Women. https://bit.ly/383bcEA

Frank, Julia. "Emma Watson goes to Uruguay to promote more women in politics." *Vogue Australia*, September 18, 2014. https://bit.ly/3dE1Q3x

"Goodwill Ambassadors." UN Women. https://bit.ly/31oM8GT

"Launch of the HeForShe Campaign." UN Web TV. https://bit.ly/2YBaAD5

"On visit to Uruguay, UN Women Goodwill Ambassador Emma Watson urges women's political participation." UN Women. https://bit.ly/2NzSxa0

"Press release: UN Women Goodwill Ambassador Emma Watson calls out to men and boys to join HeForShe campaign." UN Women. https://bit.ly/31x5GsX

Teather, Charlie. "Emma Watson on style priorities, fashion as a feminist issue and why now, at 25, she is only just feeling comfortable in her own skin." *Evening Standard*, November 30, 2015. https://bit.ly/2ZerfeY

"UN Women Goodwill Ambassador Emma Watson." UN Women. https://bit.ly/3dDRuAs

CHAPTER 1

Fahnestock, Jeanne. *Rhetorical Style: The Uses of Language in Persuasion*. New York: Oxford University, 2011.

McIntyre, Catherine. "Why do men make more money than women?" *Maclean's*, February 8, 2018. https://bit.ly/3eC3P9V

"Primary Sources." University of California Irving Libraries. https://bit.ly/3dCwKcn

"Primary Sources: What Are They?" Teaching History. https://bit.ly/31oLQjh

"Primary vs. Secondary Sources." BMCC Library. lib1.bmcc.cuny.edu/help/sources

"Using Primary Sources." United States Library of Congress. https://bit.ly/2ZbqsLL

Weida, Stacy and Karl Stolley. "Using Rhetorical Strategies for Persuasion." Purdue Online Writing Lab. https://bit.ly/2VnDLHR

CHAPTER 2

"Child Marriage Around the World." Girls Not Brides. https://bit.ly/2CFjsit

@EmmaWatson. "@lordvoldemot @HeforShe Become an engineer." *Twitter*, January 23, 2015. https://bit.ly/2BLvSFm

"Emma Watson | HeForShe Second Year Anniversary Remarks." YouTube. www.youtube.com/watch?v=N6AK6tN2P-o&t=213s

Kingdon, Victoria. "Emma Watson speaks on the 2nd anniversary of the #HeForShe campaign." *Harper's Bazaar*, September 21, 2016. https://bit.ly/2YzkRQj

"UN Women launches next phase in 'HeForShe' campaign at Davos Forum." Office of the Secretary-General's Envoy on Youth. https://bit.ly/384KhIu

CHAPTER 3

Abbruzzese, Jason. "Emma Watson Q&A on Women's Day: 'If you stand for equality, then you're a feminist.'" Mashable. https://bit.ly/3dE2myv

"An Insight, An Idea with Malala Yousafzai." World Economic Forum. https://bit.ly/3eD7q7y

Bruce-Lockhart, Anna. "Justin Trudeau tells Davos to call time on women's inequality." World Economic Forum. https://bit.ly/3dxlhL7

Chainey, Ross. "Malala in Davos: We need to teach boys to be men." World Economic Forum. https://bit.ly/2YzH3JW

"Emma Watson's UN speech: what our reaction says about feminism." The Conversation. https://bit.ly/3eFrjL9

"Feminism." History.com. https://bit.ly/3g2Ay8x

"Justin Trudeau's Davos address in full." World Economic Forum. https://bit.ly/3eFrrdB

Malala Fund. https://malala.org

"Malala Yousafzai: Biographical." The Nobel Prize. https://bit.ly/3g4KqOS

McCarthy, Amy. "Sorry Privileged White Ladies, But Emma Watson Isn't a ' Game Changer' for Feminism." *xoJane*, September 26, 2014. https://bit.ly/2NueDL8

Parker, Ceri. "'I'm a feminist,' Malala tells Emma Watson." World Economic Forum. https://bit.ly/2VmLuWw

Rezaian, Jason. "Malala has a message for Trump on women's rights." *The Washington Post*, January 25, 2018.

Samuelson, Kate. "Malala Yousafzai Accepts Honorary Canadian Citizenship." *Time*, April 13, 2017. https://bit.ly/2Nv1CB9

"Trudeau uses Davos speech to tout women's rights." Global News. https://bit.ly/3fYVhKr

Watson, Emma. "Part One: HeForShe Conversation with Emma." Facebook, March 8, 2015. https://bit.ly/2Yz1AOR

CHAPTER 4

Burrell, Ian. "Emma Watson: Speaking out about feminism opened a 'Pandora's Box' of threats and criticism, actress reveals." *Independent*, October 3, 2016. https://bit.ly/3g0Ys4b

"Emma Watson on Gender Equality and the Struggles of Activism: Transcript." *Newsweek*, September 30, 2016. https://bit.ly/384KY4y

"Press release: Ahead of International Women's Day, new UN Women report warns that progress towards gender equality is lagging and hard-fought gains are under threat." UN Women. https://bit.ly/386xi9y

"Remarks on International Women's Day 2019." United Nations Secretary-General. https://bit.ly/31he2ER

"The HeForShe Baton Launches—First Stop New York City." HeForShe. https://bit.ly/2Vk71PS

"United Nations observance of International Women's Day 2019." UN Women. https://bit.ly/384YVzv

LEARNING MORE

BOOKS

Custance, Petrice. *Emma Watson*. St. Catharines: Crabtree Publishing, 2018.

Hopkinson, Deborah. *What Is the Women's Rights Movement?* New York: Penguin Workshop, 2018.

Polak, Monique. *I Am a Feminist: Claiming the F-Word in Turbulent Times*. Victoria: Orca Book Publishers, 2019.

Sjonger, Rebecca. *Taking Action to Achieve Equality*. St. Catharines: Crabtree Publishing, 2018.

Yousafzai, Malala and Patricia McCormick. *I Am Malala: How One Girl Stood Up for Education and Changed the World*. New York: Little, Brown Books for Young Readers, 2014.

WEBSITES

Learn more about HeForShe on its official website:
www.heforshe.org/en

Get the facts about the UN's Sustainable Development Goal for Gender Equality:
www.un.org/sustainabledevelopment/gender-equality

Check out the Activist Hub of Plan International's Girls Get Equal:
plan-international.org/girls-get-equal/activist-hub

Find out about International Women's Day events:
www.internationalwomensday.com

VIDEO

Watch HeForShe approved videos:
www.youtube.com/user/heforshe

The website addresses (URLs) included in this book were valid at the time of going to press. However, it is possible that contents or addresses may have changed since the publication of this book. No responsibility for any such changes can be accepted by either the author or the Publisher.

GLOSSARY

address A speech written or directed to a specific group of people
ambassador Someone who officially represents a country in another country
analogy A similarity between two things from which a comparison is made
analyze To examine critically to understand causes and meaning
argument A discussion or debate involving different points of view
biases Opinions in favor of or against a person, group, or thing, usually in an unfair way
credibility How believable something is
critical Skillful judgment of truth and value
discrimination Judging a person based on the group or class that person belongs to, rather than on merit
economy The resources of a community or country and how they are managed
equal pay The idea that employers pay women and men equal pay for work of equal value
fundamentalist Someone who believes in the strict interpretation of a religion or idea
gender inequality The idea that men and women are not equal as humans
gender norms The standards that define what is considered acceptable or appropriate behavior or actions for people or different genders
General Assembly The main governing and decision-making part of the United Nations
human rights The basic rights and freedoms that belong to everyone from birth to death
hyperbole Obvious and intentional exaggeration
intended Designed or meant for a particular reason or purpose
Library of Congress The research library of the United States Congress that also serves as a national library
metaphor A figure of speech in which a term or phrase is used to represent something else
notable Worthy of attention or notice
personification Giving human qualities to an animal, object, or idea
persuasion Convincing or urging someone to do something by appealing to reason
persuasive Intended to persuade
poverty Lacking the necessities of life or a secure income to meet your needs
privileged Having special unearned advantages or opportunities
reproductive rights The rights of people to decide whether to have or not have children
second-class A division of people that has lower social or economic privilege
simile A figure of speech in which two things that are not alike are compared
social media Electronic communication and digital tools that allow users to communicate with online communities
solidarity People united in groups with common causes, interests, and actions
statistics Information and data that is collected and analyzed to predict or understand something
transgender People whose gender identity differs from their sex

INDEX

ABOUT THE AUTHOR

Rebecca Sjonger is the author of over 50 non-fiction books for young people. American history is one of her favorite subjects to write about. She loves the challenge of separating facts from fiction while researching.